MIGHTY MACHINES
RESCUE!

Splash!

written by Amy Johnson

MILES KELLY

Illustrated by Steven Wood

To the rescue!

If there's an emergency, there are many kinds of vehicles that may come to help!

Engines **ROAR**...

fire engine

Police patrol

On the go and on the look-out, these vehicles help the police do their jobs.

Dog unit car

Mobile command centre

Motorbike

Traffic car

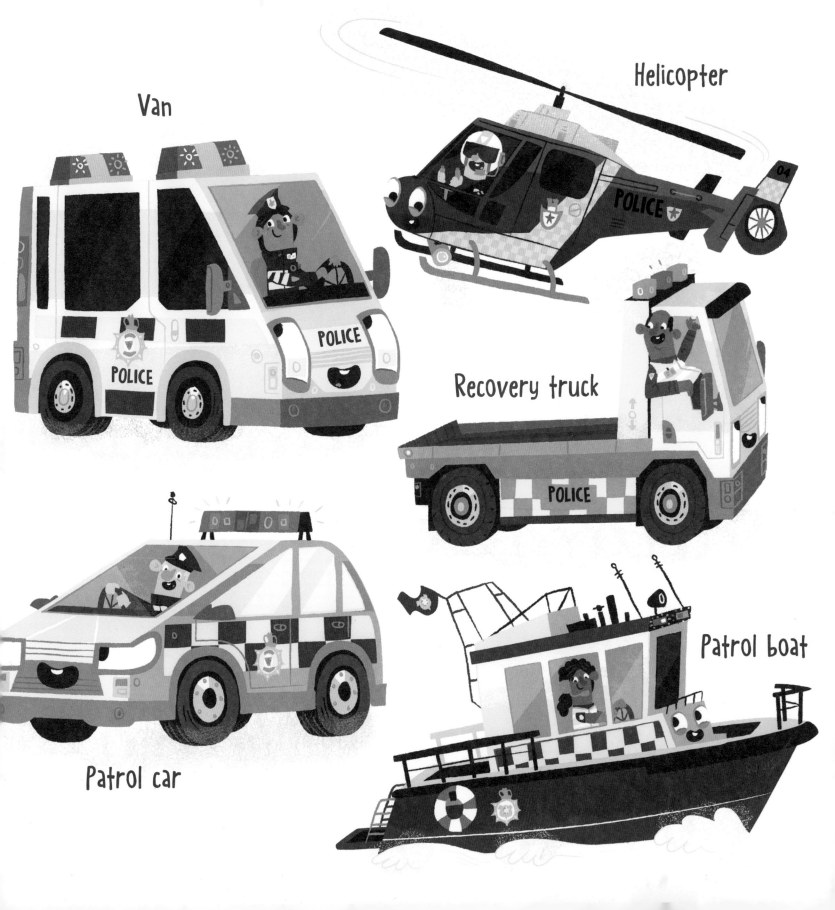

Van

Helicopter

Recovery truck

Patrol car

Patrol boat

All about lifeboats

When people get into trouble on the water, a lifeboat will head out to help them.

The aerial picks up signals so the crew can talk to the lifeboat station and other boats

Offshore lifeboats are used at sea. They're built to be speedy and to handle strong winds and waves

Y-166

RNLI-1

Big lifeboats carry a smaller one for rescues in shallow water

The lifeboat can quickly right itself if it capsizes! It has special water tanks that weigh the bottom of the boat down.

The boat sits low in the water so people can be easily reached

The hull (body) of the boat is very strong

SPLASH!

Ambulance in action

If someone is sick or injured, an **ambulance** must be able to reach them in super-quick time.

Rapid response car

I carry machines and medicine to look after the patient until the ambulance arrives.

A rapid response car can often get to an emergency even more quickly than an ambulance.

Speedy **paramedic motorcycles** can nip through traffic or along narrow roads. They are often first on the scene.

Paramedic motorcycle

Ambulance

Once the **ambulance** arrives, the paramedics get ready to move the patient onboard.

Airport emergency

Planes carry tonnes of fuel, so a fire onboard is especially dangerous. Airport fire trucks can race to the rescue in minutes. They carry crew, equipment and huge amounts of water and foam.

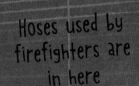

4

Water and foam are stored in here

Hoses used by firefighters are in here

Nozzles under the truck can put out fire on the ground

The cabin can fit five crew members

This sharp nozzle can punch through the wall of a plane. It is attached to an extra-long arm

WHOOSH!

Nozzles spray foam to smother the fire

The heavy truck has six wheels

Busy machines!

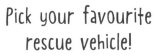

Pick your favourite rescue vehicle!

Mountain rescue

Some climbers are lost in the mountains! A search and rescue crew gets to work to track them down.

Offroad trucks can take on steep, slippery ground. They carry stretchers and first aid kits.

A minibus carries rescuers and equipment.

Blades whirring, the **helicopter** searches from above. Suddenly, it gets the call – the climbers have been spotted!

I hover in the air and lift people to safety using a winch.

AMBULANCE

Quad bikes can speed over all kinds of tricky ground.

All about ambulances

It's the job of an **ambulance** to get sick or injured people to hospital as fast as possible.

Sirens and flashing lights warn other vehicles to give way

The crew use a radio to talk to the control centre or hospital

Ambulances have bright markings or symbols so they can be easily seen

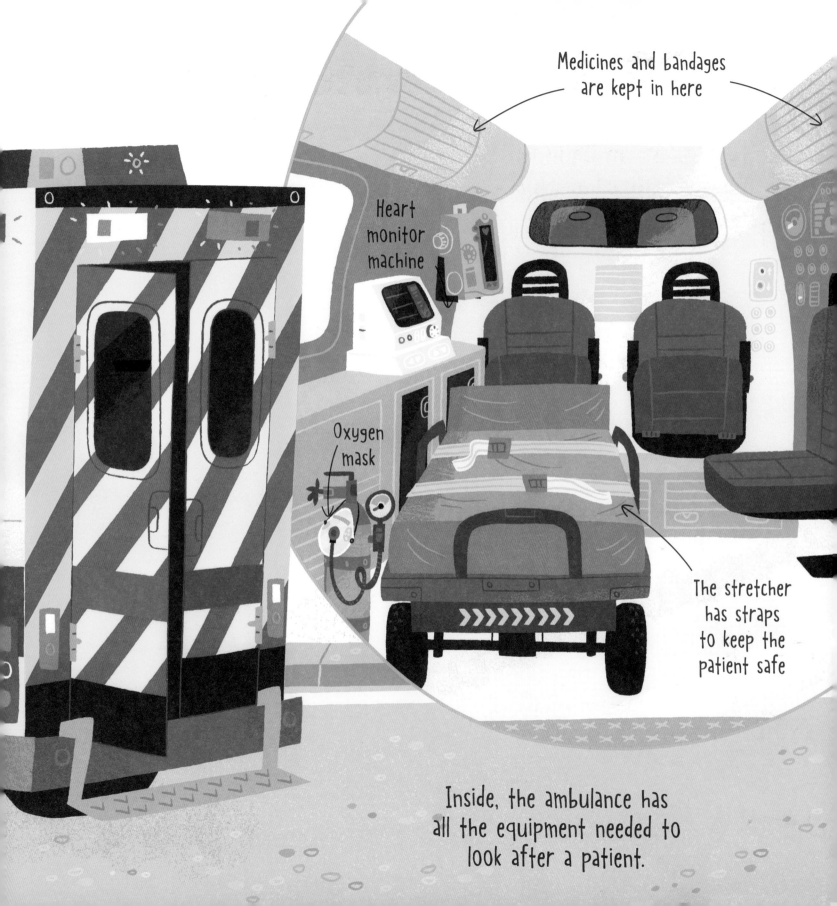

Medicines and bandages are kept in here

Heart monitor machine

Oxygen mask

The stretcher has straps to keep the patient safe

Inside, the ambulance has all the equipment needed to look after a patient.

On the water

Climb aboard! On rivers, at the coast and further out to sea, there are rescue vessels ready to help.

Offshore lifeboat

RNLI-11

Inshore lifeboat

B-756

Rescue hovercraft

Lifeguard rescue boat

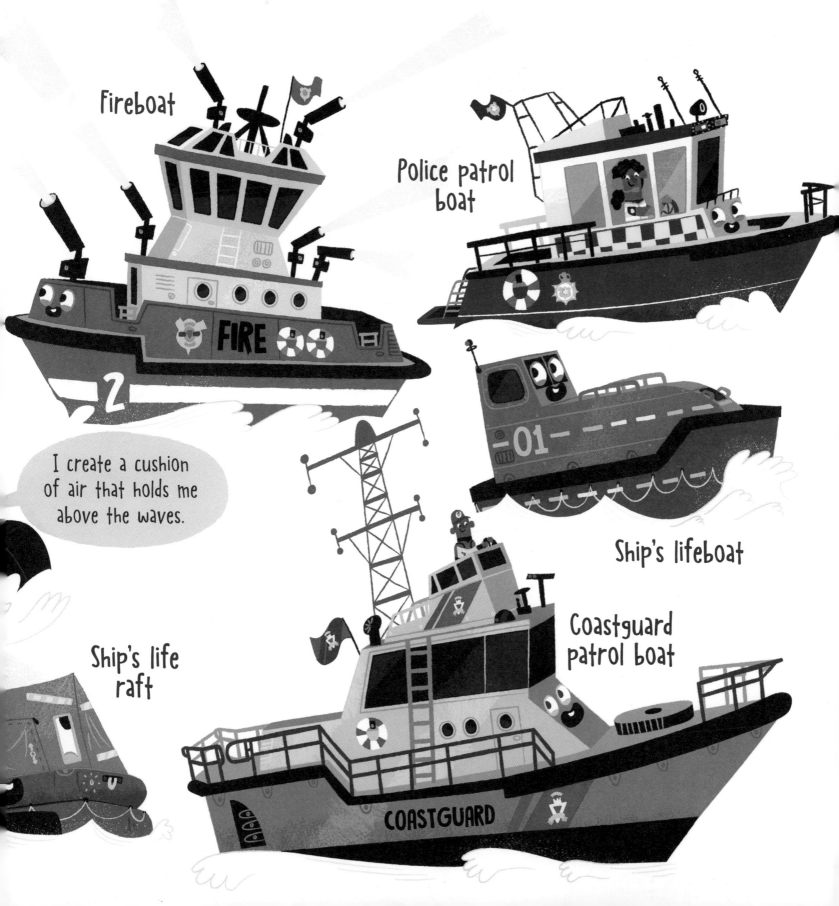

Fighting fire

A fire is blazing, flames crackle and spark, but the fire engines are on the scene!

Firefighters work from the platform

Ladder trucks have an extra-long ladder that slides up to tackle flames in tall buildings.

Legs to keep the truck steady

Hose

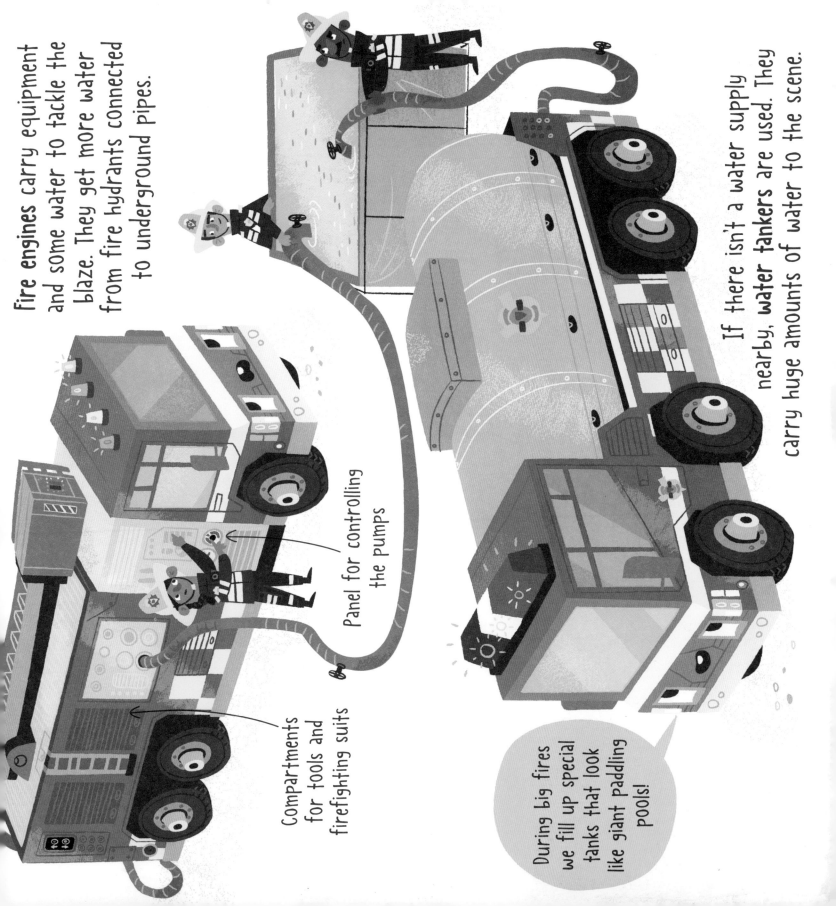

Fire engines carry equipment and some water to tackle the blaze. They get more water from fire hydrants connected to underground pipes.

If there isn't a water supply nearby, water tankers are used. They carry huge amounts of water to the scene.

Panel for controlling the pumps

Compartments for tools and firefighting suits

During big fires we fill up special tanks that look like giant paddling pools!

Rescue flight

An air ambulance helicopter can reach sick or injured people and get them quickly to hospital.

Firefighting planes drop water and special chemicals ahead of forest fires to stop them spreading.

Search and rescue helicopters find people in trouble and make daring rescues.

Police helicopters help track down suspects, search for missing people, and keep an eye on big crowds.

It's easy for me to keep up with a speedy suspect!

Snow searcher

Tough all-terrain vehicles are often used to rescue people stranded in heavy snow.

There is room inside for 17 people

I'm great at snowy search and rescue as I don't get stuck.

Two sections joined together move over drifts and slopes more easily

Wide, tough tracks stop the vehicle sinking